This book
belongs to

What Katy Did

BY

SUSAN COOLIDGE

ADAPTED BY MARC D. FALKOFF

❈

HARPERFESTIVAL®

A Division of HarperCollins*Publishers*

What Katy Did was first published in 1872.

HarperCollins®, ®, and HarperFestival® are registered trademarks
of HarperCollins Publishers Inc.

For information address HarperCollins Children's Books, a division of HarperCollins Publishers, 10 East 53rd Street, New York, NY 10022.

Library of Congress Cataloging-in-Publication Data
Coolidge, Susan, 1835–1905.
What Katy did / Susan Coolidge ; adapted by Marc D. Falkoff.
p. cm.
Summary: Twelve-year-old Katy always planned to do a great many wonderful things but in the end did something she never planned at all.
ISBN 0-694-01283-1
[1. Family life—Fiction. 2. Sick—Fiction.] I. Falkoff, Marc D. II. Title.
PZ7.C67759Wh 1999 98-41709
[Fic]—DC21 CIP
AC

Typography by Fritz Metsch
1 2 3 4 5 6 7 8 9 10
❖
First Chapter Book Charmers edition, 1999

Visit us on the World Wide Web!
http://www.harperchildrens.com

CONTENTS

❈

What Katy Did

[1]

The Little Carrs

❖

THERE ONCE WAS a girl whose name was Katy Carr. She lived in a large house on the edge of a small town. The house was white, with green blinds, and had a porch in front surrounded by roses. On one side of the house was an orchard, and on the other side were woodpiles and barns. Behind was a pasture with a brook in it.

There were six Carr children—four girls and two boys. Katy, the oldest, was twelve. Little Phil, the youngest, was four, and the rest fit in between.

Dr. Carr, their papa, was a dear, kind, busy man, who was away from home all day, and sometimes all night, too, taking care of sick people. The children didn't have a mama. She had died when Phil was a baby.

In place of this mama, there was Aunt Izzie, Papa's sister, who came to take care of them. Aunt Izzie was a small woman, sharp-faced and thin, and very particular about everything. Aunt Izzie thought children should be neat and quiet and good—as she had been.

"Clover, go upstairs and wash your hands! Dorry, pick your hat off the floor and hang it on the nail! Johnnie, make your bed this instant!" These were the kinds of things Aunt Izzie said all day long. The children minded her pretty well, but they didn't exactly love her.

One day, five out of the six Carr children were sitting along the top of a fence. Clover, the second oldest, sat in the middle. She was a sweet girl, with thick pigtails of light brown hair and blue eyes that always seemed ready to cry. Really, Clover was the jolliest little thing in the world. But those eyes always made people feel like petting her and taking her part, especially Katy.

Little Phil sat on the fence next to Clover, who held him tight with her arm. Then came Elsie, a thin, brown girl of eight, with beautiful dark eyes and crisp, short curls covering the whole of her head. All Elsie wanted was to be allowed to go about with Katy and Clover and to know their secrets. But Katy didn't want Elsie about and used to tell her to "run away and play with the children," which hurt her feelings very much.

Dorry and Joanna sat at the end of the fence. Dorry was six years old and a pale, pudgy boy, with smears of molasses on the sleeve of his jacket. Joanna, whom the children called "Johnnie," was a year younger than Dorry. She had big eyes and a wide rosy mouth, which always looked ready to laugh.

And now, as they all sat there chattering and giggling, the window opened, and Katy's head appeared. "Hurray!" she cried. "Come on, let's go!"

Clover fetched a couple of baskets from the woodshed. Elsie ran for her kitten. Dorry and Johnnie loaded themselves with two great blankets. Just as they were ready, the side door banged, and Katy came into the yard.

Katy looked as wild as ever in the afternoon sun. Her hair, as usual, was in a tangle, and her dress was a bit torn from always being caught on nails and things. Katy was the *longest* girl that was ever seen. Sometimes she felt as if she were all legs and elbows, and angles and joints. She was a dear, loving girl, for all her careless habits, and made bushels of good resolutions every week of her life, only unluckily she never kept any of them.

[2]

Paradise

❈

THE CHILDREN WERE going to a marshy thicket at the bottom of the field near the house. The children called this place "Paradise," and to them it seemed as wide and endless and full of adventure as any forest or fairyland.

The way to Paradise was through a wooden fence. Katy and Clover climbed over it, while the smaller ones scrambled underneath. Once past the fence they were in the field, and they all began to run till they reached the entrance of the wood. Then they all stopped. It was always exciting to go to Paradise for the first time after the long winter. Who knew what the fairies might have done since they had last been there?

In they marched, Katy heading the procession, and Dorry bringing up the rear.

"Oh, there is dear Rosy Posy, all safe!" cried the children, as they reached the top of the hill and came upon a wild rose bush. They were always inventing stories about this "Rosy Posy" and were always afraid that some hungry cow had come by to eat it up.

"Yes," said Katy, "it was in great danger one night last winter, but it escaped."

"Oh! How? Tell us about it!" cried the others, for Katy's stories were famous in the family.

"It was Christmas Eve," said Katy, in a mysterious tone. "The rose fairy was quite sick with a cold in her head. So she made a large acorn-cup full of tea, and then fell asleep. In the middle of the night, when she was snoring soundly, there was a noise in the forest, and a dreadful black bull with fiery eyes galloped up. He saw our poor Rosy Posy, and opening his big mouth, he was just going to bite her in two. But at that minute a little fat man, with a wand in his hand, popped out from behind the rose bush. It was Santa Claus, of course. He gave the bull such a rap with his wand that he mooed dreadfully and galloped off as fast as he could into the woods. Then Santa Claus woke up the fairy and told her that if she didn't take better care of Rosy Posy he would put some other fairy into her place."

All the children gasped at the thought.

Then Dorry said, "I'm getting hungry."

In fact, they all were, so they spread out the blankets

and gathered around Katy, who lifted the lid of the largest basket. Everyone peeped eagerly to see what was inside.

First came a great many ginger cakes. These were carefully laid on the grass to keep for later. Buttered biscuits came next—three apiece, with slices of cold lamb laid in between. And last of all were a dozen hard-boiled eggs and a layer of thick bread and butter sandwiched with corned beef. Aunt Izzie had made lunches for trips to Paradise before and knew pretty well what everyone wanted.

Oh, how good everything tasted out of doors, with the fresh wind rustling the leaves, with sunshine and sweet wood smells about them, and with birds singing overhead! When the last crumb had vanished, Katy took out the second basket, and there—oh, delightful surprise!—were six little molasses pies, each with a brown top and crisp, candied edge.

Everyone shouted at once. Six pairs of hands were held out at once toward the basket, and six sets of teeth went to work without a moment's delay, until every last crumb had disappeared.

Now that lunch was finished and the children rested, games of chase and tag and hide-and-seek began. The Carr children spent all the afternoon running about, but it seemed as if only a minute had passed before the long shadows began to fall and they had to go back inside to get ready for dinner. It was dreadful to have to pick up the empty baskets and go home, but it was comforting to remember that Paradise would always be there for them another day.

[3]

The Day of Scrapes

❈

KATY AND CLOVER went to Mrs. Knight's school, a low building with a yard behind it in which the girls played at recess. Next door was Miss Miller's school, which also had a yard behind. Only a high board fence separated the two playgrounds. The "Knights" and the "Millerites" were archrivals.

The students spent their recesses mostly in making faces through the knotholes in the fence. But the Knight girls had one great advantage: in their yard was a woodshed, with a climbable roof, and upon this the girls used to sit in rows, turning up their noses at the Millerites in the next yard.

One morning, not long after the day in Paradise, Katy was late. She could not find her things. Her algebra had gone and lost itself, her slate was missing, and the string was off her sunbonnet. She ran about, searching for these things and banging doors, till Aunt Izzie was out of patience.

"As for your algebra book," Aunt Izzie said, "if it is that very dirty book with only one cover, you will find it under the kitchen table. How you manage to spoil your schoolbooks in this manner, Katy, I cannot imagine. About your slate, I know nothing. But there is your bonnet string, by the flowers."

"Oh, thank you!" said Katy, hastily sticking it on with a pin.

"Katy Carr!" cried Miss Izzie. "What *are* you doing? Pinning on your bonnet string! Mercy! Now stand still and don't fidget. Don't move till I have sewed it on properly."

It wasn't easy to stand still and not fidget, but Katy bore it as well as she could, only now and then uttering a little snort, like an antsy horse. The minute she was released she flew outside to where Clover was waiting for her.

"We shall have to run," gasped Katy. "Aunt Izzie kept me. She's been so horrid!"

They did run as fast as they could, but before they were halfway to school the town clock struck nine, and they knew they were late.

"There," Katy said. "I shall just tell Aunt Izzie that it

was her fault." And she marched into school in a very cross mood.

After that, everything went wrong. Katy twice made mistakes in her grammar lesson, and her hand shook so when she copied her composition that Mrs. Knight said it must be done all over again. This made Katy crosser than ever. As soon as the bell rang for recess, she climbed up all alone to the woodshed roof. There she sat with her back to the school, fighting with her eyes not to cry.

Miss Miller's clock was about four minutes slower than Mrs. Knight's, so the other playground was empty. It was a warm, breezy day, and as Katy sat there, suddenly a gust of wind came and blew her sunbonnet across the roof. It disappeared over the edge, and Katy, flying after, saw it lying in the very middle of the enemy's yard.

This was horrible! In another minute the Miller girls would be out. Already Katy seemed to see them dancing war dances around the unfortunate bonnet, pinning it on a pole and waving it over the fence. Was it to be endured? Never! So Katy set her teeth and, sliding rapidly down the roof, seized the fence and jumped down into Miss Miller's yard.

Just then the recess bell rang, and a little Millerite cried out, "There's Katy Carr in our backyard!"

Out poured the Millerites, big and little. With a howl of fury, they went after Katy, but she was as quick as they were, and holding her bonnet in her hand, she scrambled back up the fence.

There are moments when it is a fine thing to be tall. In one second she was over the top of the fence. Then a shout of victory went up from the Knights: "Hurrah for Katy Carr!"

Katy was kissed and hugged and made to tell the story of her adventure over and over again. Altogether it was a great day for the school, a day to be remembered.

That noon, after they had eaten their lunches, Katy suggested to the girls that they play a new game she had invented, called "the Game of Rivers."

These were the rules. Each girl took the name of a river, then laid out for herself a path through the room, winding among the desks and benches and making a low, roaring sound, like the noise of water. They had to run into each other once in a while because, as Katy said, "rivers do." As for Katy herself, she was "Father Ocean" and, growling horribly, raged up and down the entire room. Every now and then, Katy would suddenly cry out, "Now for a meeting of the waters!" whereupon all the rivers would turn and run toward Father Ocean, while he roared louder than all of them put together and rushed up and down, much like the waves on a beach.

Such a noise as this beautiful game made was never heard before or since. People going by the school stopped and stared, babies cried, and an old lady asked why someone didn't call the police.

Mrs. Knight, coming back from lunch, was amazed to see a crowd of people in front of her school. As she drew near, the sounds reached her, and then she became really frightened. Hurrying in, she threw open the door and saw chairs flung down, desks upset, ink streaming on the floor, and in the middle of this ruin was Katy Carr, with a face as red as fire, roaring out her role as Father Ocean.

"*What* is going on here?" cried poor Mrs. Knight.

At the sound of her voice, each girl realized what a condition the room was in, and how naughty they'd been.

When all was in order again and the girls had taken their seats, Mrs. Knight made a short speech. She said she had never been so shocked in her life. All the girls would have to be punished, but if anyone felt that she was more to blame than the others, now was the moment to confess it.

Katy's heart gave a great thump, but she rose bravely. "I made up the game, and I was Father Ocean," she said to Mrs. Knight, who stared at her for a minute.

"Very well, Katy. Sit down." Katy did, feeling more ashamed than ever, but somehow relieved in her mind.

Mrs. Knight began to scold them, and before long most of the girls began to cry. Their punishment was to be the loss of recess for three weeks.

After this lecture, Mrs. Knight called Katy up to her desk and said a few words to her specially. She was not really severe, but before long Katy was weeping like the ocean she had pretended to be.

At this, Mrs. Knight was so touched that she let her off at once and even kissed her in forgiveness, which made poor Ocean sob harder than ever.

That evening Dr. Carr was at home. It was always a great treat to the children when this happened, and Katy thought herself happy when, after the little ones had gone to bed, she got Papa to herself and told him the whole story.

"Papa," she said, sitting on his knee, "what is the reason that makes some days so lucky and other days so unlucky? Now, today began all wrong, and everything that happened in it was wrong. On other days I begin right, and all goes right straight through. If Aunt Izzie hadn't kept me in the morning I shouldn't have been late, and then I shouldn't have been cross, and then *perhaps* I shouldn't have got in my other scrapes."

"But what made Aunt Izzie keep you, Katy?"

"To sew on the string of my bonnet, Papa."

"But how did it happen that the string was off?"

"Well," said Katy, "I am afraid that was my fault, for it came off on Tuesday, and I didn't sew it on."

"So you see, we must go further back than Aunt Izzie

for the beginning of this unlucky day of yours, Katy."

"Oh, Papa," cried Katy, giving him a great hug as she got off his knee, "I see what you mean! Who would have thought such a little thing as not sewing on my string could make such a big difference? But I don't believe I shall get in any more trouble, for I'll never forget this day of scrapes."

[4]

Kikeri

❈

BUT POOR, THOUGHTLESS Katy *did* forget.

One evening, Aunt Izzie decided to go to a lecture. Before she left, she wondered if it was really wise to leave Katy in charge.

"How do I know," she asked Katy, "that before I come home you won't have set the house on fire or killed somebody?"

"Oh, no, we won't!" cried Katy.

"Well," said Aunt Izzie, unconvinced, "I won't be back late. See that all the children are in bed by nine."

"Yes'm," said Katy. But she was *really* thinking about how jolly it was to have Aunt Izzie go out for once. Aunt Izzie almost never left the children alone, so whenever she did, they felt a certain sense of freedom.

Still, Katy meant no mischief. She seldom did *mean* to

do wrong—she just did it when it came into her head. In fact, all might have gone well if one of the children hadn't suggested a game of "Kikeri."

Kikeri was a game the Carr children had invented themselves. It was a mixture of blindman's buff and tag—only, instead of using a blindfold, everyone played in the dark. One of the children would stay out in the hall, which was lighted from the stairs, while the others hid themselves in the dark nursery. When they were all hidden, they would call out "Kikeri!" as a signal for the one in the hall to come in and find them. Of course, coming from the light he could see nothing, while the others could see only dimly. It was very exciting to stand crouching up in a corner and watch as the "finder" stumbled about, while every now and then somebody would slip past and get to the hall to safety, shouting "Kikeri! Kikeri! Kikeri!" Whoever was caught had to take the place of the finder.

For a long time this game was the delight of the Carr children. But so many scratches and black-and-blue spots came of it that at last Aunt Izzie ordered that they should not play it anymore.

"But we didn't *promise*," said Dorry.

"No, and Papa never said a word about our not playing it," added Katy.

So they all went downstairs and began the game.

It was splendid fun. Once Clover climbed up on the mantelpiece and sat there, and when Katy, who was finder, groped about a little more wildly than usual, she caught hold of Clover's foot and couldn't imagine where it came from. The fun and frolic seemed to grow greater the longer they played. In the excitement, time went by faster than any of them dreamed. Suddenly, they heard a door slam. Aunt Izzie had returned from her lecture!

What confusion! They all scattered to their bedrooms.

Katy went to bed with all possible speed. But the others were not as nimble. Dorry and Phil popped into bed half undressed. Elsie disappeared into her trundle bed without even pulling it out! And Clover fell on her knees with her face buried in a chair, pretending to pray.

Aunt Izzie came in with a candle in her hand. She waited and waited for Clover to finish. At last she said, "That will do, Clover, you can get up."

Aunt Izzie began at once to undress her, and while doing so asked a great many questions, and before long she had got at the truth of the whole matter. She went to the beds where Phil and Dorry lay snoring as loudly as they knew how. But something strange in the appearance of the beds made her look more closely. She lifted the covers, and there, sure enough, she saw that Phil and Dorry were wearing their shoes!

Such a scolding Aunt Izzie gave the little scamps! She

dressed them for bed and tucked them warmly in. Then she asked, "Where is my poor little Elsie?"

"In bed," said Dorry.

"In bed!" said Aunt Izzie. Stooping down, she gave a pull and the trundle bed came into view. And sure enough, there was Elsie, fully dressed, shoes and all, but fast asleep. She was the only one of the children who did not get the scolding she deserved that night.

Katy did not even pretend to be asleep when Aunt Izzie went to her room. She was lying in bed, very miserable at having gotten the others into trouble as well as herself. And she knew that she'd failed to set an example to the younger ones.

The next day, Dr. Carr talked to her more seriously than he had ever done before. Poor Katy! She sobbed as if her heart would break at this, and though she made no promises, she was never so thoughtless again after that day.

As for the rest, Papa called them together and made them understand that Kikeri was never to be played anymore. And this time they obeyed.

[5]

Cousin Helen's Visit

❈

SOON IT WAS summer. School was over, and all the Carr children had to do was run around outside, visit Paradise every day, and get as rosy and plump as strawberries. Dr. Carr believed that nothing was better for growing children than fresh air and plenty of activity.

One afternoon, Katy and Clover came running through the front door and raced each other upstairs. Then they stopped short, for the upper hall was all in confusion. Sounds of dusting and cleaning came from the spare room. Tables and chairs were standing about, and a cot-bed stood at the top of the stairs.

"Why, what's going on?" asked Katy. "Oh, Aunt Izzie, who's coming?"

"Oh, gracious! Is that you?" replied Aunt Izzie, who looked very hot and flurried. "Now, children, it's no use for you to stand there asking questions. I haven't got time to answer them. Go right downstairs, both of you, and don't come up this way again till after tea. I'm much too busy to talk right now."

"Just tell us what's going to happen, and we will," cried the children.

"Your Cousin Helen is coming to visit us," said Aunt Izzie, and disappeared upstairs.

This was news indeed! The children had heard a lot about Cousin Helen, but they had never met her. She had become much like a character in a fairy story to them.

They knew that Cousin Helen was ill, and that she had once been in an accident and would never be able to walk about on her own again. She had to lie on a sofa all the time. Papa always went to visit her twice a year, and he liked to talk to the children about her and tell how sweet and patient she was, and what a pretty room she lived in.

"What do you suppose she looks like?" Clover asked Katy as they went downstairs.

"Oh, she has blue eyes, I'd guess, and curls. And a long, straight nose. And she'll keep her hands clasped all the time and lie on the sofa perfectly still and never smile, but just look patient. And she reads the Bible and sings hymns all day long," said Katy, who was trying to imagine how an angel would look and behave.

The time seemed very long till five o'clock, when Cousin Helen was expected. The children all sat on the steps waiting for the carriage, until at last it drove up. Papa motioned to the children to stand back. Then he carefully lifted Cousin Helen in his arms and brought her in.

"Oh, there are the chicks!" were the first words the children heard, in such a gay, pleasant voice. "Do set me down somewhere, Uncle. I want to see them so much!"

So Papa put Cousin Helen on the hall sofa.

"Cousin Helen wants to see you," he called to the children.

"Indeed I do," said the bright voice. "So this is Katy? Why, what a splendid tall Katy it is! And this is Clover," kissing her. "And this dear little Elsie. You all look as natural as possible—just as if I had seen you before." And she hugged all of them as if she had loved them and known them all her life.

There was something in Cousin Helen's face which made the children at home with her at once. Still, Katy's first feeling was one of disappointment. Cousin Helen did not look *exactly* like an angel. She had brown hair, which didn't curl, and bright eyes that danced when she laughed or spoke. She didn't fold her hands, and she didn't look patient. But the more Katy watched Cousin

Helen, the more she liked her and felt as if she were much merrier than the imaginary person that she had invented.

"She looks just like other people, doesn't she?" whispered Clover.

"Y-e-s," replied Katy, "only a great deal prettier."

By and by Papa carried Cousin Helen upstairs. All the children wanted to go too, but he told them she was tired and needed to rest. So they went outdoors to play till teatime.

"Oh, do let me take up the tray," cried Katy at the tea table as she watched Aunt Izzie getting ready Cousin Helen's supper. Such a nice supper of cold chicken, raspberries and cream, and tea in a pretty pink-and-white china cup.

"No indeed," said Aunt Izzie. "You'll drop it the first thing." But Katy's eyes begged so hard that Dr. Carr said, "Yes, let her, Izzie."

So Katy took the tray and carried it carefully across the hall. There was a bowl of flowers on the table. As she passed, she set down the tray, picked out a rose, and laid it on the napkin beside the saucer of raspberries. It looked very pretty, and Katy smiled to herself with pleasure.

Then she sped upstairs as fast as she could go. She had just reached the door of Cousin Helen's room when she tripped over her bootlace—which was untied, as usual—and stumbled. The door flew open, and Katy—with the tray, cream, raspberries, rose, and all—fell in a heap upon the carpet.

Cousin Helen, in bed, was of course a good deal startled at the sudden crash and tumble on her floor. But nothing could have been sweeter than the way in which she comforted poor crestfallen Katy, and she made so merry over the accident that even Aunt Izzie almost forgot to scold. The broken dishes were piled up, and the carpet made clean again, while Aunt Izzie prepared another tray just as nice as the first.

"Please let Katy bring it up!" Cousin Helen asked Aunt Izzie, who wrinkled her brow at this. "I am sure she will be careful this time. And Katy, I want just such another rose on the napkin. That was your doing—wasn't it?"

Katy *was* careful. And this time all went well. The tray was placed safely on a little table beside the bed, and Katy sat watching Cousin Helen eat with a warm, loving feeling at her heart.

The next morning all the children went into Cousin Helen's room. Such a merry morning as they had! Cousin Helen was a wonderful storyteller and came up with loads of new games that could be played near her sofa. Aunt Izzie, dropping in about eleven o'clock, found them having such a good time that, almost before she knew it, *she* was drawn into a game, too. Nobody had ever heard of such a thing before!

Clover privately thought that Cousin Helen must be a witch. And Papa, when he came home at noon, said almost the same thing.

"What have you been doing to them, Helen?" he asked as he opened the door and saw his family sitting in a circle on the carpet. Aunt Izzie's hair was half pulled down, and Philly was rolling over and over laughing. But Cousin Helen said she hadn't done anything, and pretty soon Papa was on the floor, too, playing away as fast as the rest.

"I must put a stop to this," he cried, when everybody was tired of laughing. "Cousin Helen will be worn out. Run away, all of you, and don't come near this door again till the clock strikes four. Do you hear, chicks? Run! Shoo!"

"It must be awful to be sick," thought Katy to herself as she left Cousin Helen's room. "Why, if I had to stay in bed a whole week I should *die.* I know I should."

For the next few days the children could be found in Cousin Helen's room most all the time—except for when Aunt Izzie ordered them to let their guest rest. When the last evening came, and the children went up to her room, Cousin Helen was opening a box that had just come by express.

"It's a 'Good-bye Box,'" she said.

First came a vase exactly like the one Cousin Helen kept in her room. Katy screamed with delight as it was placed in her hands.

"Oh, how lovely! How lovely!" she cried. "I'll keep it as long as I live and breathe."

Next came a pretty purple pocketbook for Clover. It was just what she wanted. Then a little locket on a bit of velvet ribbon, which Cousin Helen tied around Elsie's neck.

"There's a piece of my hair in it," she said. "Why, Elsie, darling, what's the matter? Don't cry so!"

"Oh, you're *so* beautiful, and so *sweet*!" sobbed Elsie.

Dorry got a box of dominoes, and Johnnie a solitaire board. And for Phil there was a book, *The History of the Robber Cat*.

The next day they had to say good-bye. They all stood at the gate and waved as the carriage drove away. When it was out of sight, Katy rushed off to weep a little to herself.

"Papa said he wished we were all like Cousin Helen," she thought as she wiped her eyes, "and I mean to try, though I don't suppose if I tried a thousand years I should ever get to be half so good. I'll study, and keep my things in order, and be ever so kind to the little ones. Dear me, if only Aunt Izzie were Cousin Helen, how easy it would be! Never mind. I'll think about her all the time, and I'll begin tomorrow to be good."

[6]

Tomorrow

❈

"TOMORROW I WILL begin," thought Katy as she dropped asleep that night. But when she opened her eyes, she was as fractious as a bear! The very first thing she did was to break her precious vase—the one Cousin Helen had given her.

It was standing on the bureau with a little cluster of roses in it. The bureau had a swing-mirror. While Katy was brushing her hair, the mirror tipped a little so that she could not see. Being angry, she gave the glass a violent push. The lower part swung forward, and there was a smash. The roses lay scattered all over the floor, and Cousin Helen's pretty present was ruined.

Katy just sat down on the carpet and cried as hard as if she had been Phil himself. Aunt Izzie heard her and came in.

"I'm very sorry," Aunt Izzie said, picking up the broken glass. "But it's no more than I expected, you're so careless, Katy. Now get up and dress yourself. You'll be late to breakfast."

At the breakfast table, Dr. Carr was chatting with the children. "Well, what are you chicks going to do today?" he asked.

"Swing!" cried Johnnie and Dorry together.

"No, you're not," said Aunt Izzie. "The swing is not to be used till tomorrow. Remember that, children. Not till tomorrow. And not then, unless I tell you so."

This was unwise of Aunt Izzie. It would have been better had she explained further. The truth was that the swing was not fastened to the woodshed roof properly. It could not be fixed till tomorrow, and until then it really was not safe. If she had told this to the children, all would have been right. But Aunt Izzie's theory was that young people must obey their elders without explanation.

"Katy," continued Aunt Izzie, "your top drawer is all out of order. I never saw anything look so badly. I want you to go upstairs after breakfast and straighten it before you do anything else."

After breakfast Katy went slowly upstairs. It was a warm day, her head ached a little, and her eyes felt heavy from crying so much. Everything seemed dull and hateful. She thought that Aunt Izzie was very unkind to make her work during vacation, and she pulled the top drawer open with a groan.

Aunt Izzie was right. A bureau drawer could hardly look worse than this one did. All sorts of things were mixed together. There were books and paint boxes and bits of scribbled paper and lead pencils and brushes all over the place. It took much time and patience to bring order out of this confusion. But Katy knew that Aunt Izzie would be up by and by, and she dared not stop till all was done. By the time it was finished she was very tired.

Going downstairs, she met Elsie coming up with a slate in her hand, which, as soon as she saw Katy, she put behind her.

"You mustn't look," she said. "It's my letter to Cousin Helen. It's a secret. It's all written, and I'm going to send it to the post office. See, there's a stamp on it." And she showed a corner of the slate. Sure enough, there was a stamp stuck on the frame.

"You little goose!" said Katy. "You can't send that to the post office. Here, give me the slate. I'll copy what you've written on paper, and Papa'll give you an envelope."

"No, no," cried Elsie. "You mustn't! You'll see what I've said, and it's a secret. Let go of my slate! I'll tell Cousin Helen what a mean girl you are, and then she won't love you a bit."

"There, then, take your old slate!" said Katy, giving her a little push. Elsie slipped and fell with a thump on the hall floor.

It wasn't much of a fall, but the bump was a hard one, and Elsie cried as if she had been half killed. Aunt Izzie came rushing to the spot.

"Katy—pushed—me!" cried Elsie.

"Well, Katy Carr, I should think you'd be ashamed of yourself," said Aunt Izzie. "There, there, Elsie! Don't cry any more, dear. Come upstairs with me. Katy won't hurt you again."

So they went upstairs. Katy, left below, felt very miserable. She had not meant to hurt Elsie and was ashamed of that push. But she was still too angry to admit this.

"I don't care," she murmured, choking back her tears. "Elsie is a real crybaby anyway. And Aunt Izzie always takes her side."

She went by the side door into the yard. As she passed the shed, the swing caught her eye.

"How exactly like Aunt Izzie," she thought, "ordering the children not to swing till she says so. I suppose she thinks it's too hot, or something. I won't listen to her, anyhow."

She seated herself in the swing. It was a first-rate one, with a comfortable seat and thick new ropes. It hung just the right distance from the floor, and the woodshed was the nicest possible spot in which to have it.

It was a big place, with a very high roof. There was not much wood left in it just now, and the little there was, was piled neatly about the sides of the shed so as to leave plenty of room. The place felt cool and dark, and the motion of the swing seemed to set the breeze blowing. It waved Katy's hair like a great fan and made her dreamy and quiet.

Swinging to and fro, she gradually rose higher and higher, driving herself along by the motion of her body and striking the floor smartly with her foot at every sweep. Now she was at the top of the high-arched door. Then she could almost touch the cross-beam above it, and through the small square window she could see pigeons sitting on the roof-beams. She had never swung so high before. It was like flying, she thought, as she bent in the seat, trying to send herself yet higher and graze the roof-beams with her toes.

Suddenly, at the very highest point of the sweep, there was a sharp noise of cracking. The swing gave a violent twist, spun half around, and tossed Katy into the air. She clutched the rope—felt it dragged from her grasp—then down—down—she fell. All grew dark, and she knew no more.

When she opened her eyes she was lying on the sofa in the dining room. Clover was kneeling beside her with a pale, scared face, and Aunt Izzie was placing something cold and wet on her forehead.

"What's the matter?" said Katy faintly.

"Oh, she's alive—she's alive!" and Clover put her arms around Katy's neck and sobbed.

"Hush, dear!" Aunt Izzie's voice sounded unusually gentle. "You've had a bad tumble, Katy. Don't you remember?"

"A tumble? Oh, yes—out of the swing," said Katy. "Did the rope break, Aunt Izzie? I don't remember."

"No, Katy, not the rope. The staple drew out of the roof. It was cracked, and not safe. Don't you remember my telling you not to swing today? Did you forget?"

"No, Aunt Izzie, I didn't forget. I—" but here Katy broke down. She closed her eyes, and big tears rolled from under the lids.

"Don't cry," whispered Clover, crying herself. "Please don't. Aunt Izzie isn't going to scold you." But Katy was too weak and shaken not to cry.

"I think I'd like to go upstairs and lie on the bed," she said. But when she tried to get off the sofa, everything swam before her, and she fell back again on the pillow.

"Why, I can't stand up!" Katy cried, looking very much frightened.

"I'm afraid you've given yourself a sprain somewhere," said Aunt Izzie, who looked rather frightened herself. "You'd better lie still a while, dear, before you try to move. Ah, here's the doctor now." And she went to answer the knock at the door. It was Dr. Alsop, who lived quite near.

"I am so relieved that you could come," Aunt Izzie said. "My brother has gone out of town, not to return till tomorrow, and one of the girls has had a bad fall."

Dr. Alsop sat down beside the sofa and took Katy's pulse. Then he asked, "Can you move this leg?"

Katy gave a feeble kick.

"And this?"

That kick was a good deal more feeble. "Did that hurt you?" asked Dr. Alsop, seeing the look of pain on her face.

"Yes, a little," replied Katy, trying hard not to cry.

"In your back, eh?" The doctor turned to Aunt Izzie. "You'd better get her upstairs and undress her as soon as you can, Miss Carr. I'll leave a prescription to rub her with." And Dr. Alsop took out a bit of paper and began to write.

"Oh, must I go to bed?" said Katy. "How long will I have to stay there, Doctor?"

"That depends on how fast you get well," he replied. "Not long, I hope. Maybe only a few days."

"A few days!" cried Katy.

After the doctor was gone, Aunt Izzie and Debbie, the Cook, lifted Katy and carried her slowly upstairs. It was not easy, for every motion hurt Katy, and the sense of being helpless hurt most of all. She couldn't help crying after she was undressed and put into bed.

Such a long afternoon that was! Aunt Izzie brought up some dinner, but Katy couldn't eat. Little prickles of pain ran up and down her back. She lay with her eyes shut because it hurt to keep them open.

Katy heard a light footstep, and then Elsie's soft whisper in her ear.

"Don't be frightened, Katy," said Elsie. "I won't disturb you. I'm so sorry you're sick. But we mean to keep real quiet, and never bang the nursery door or make noises on the stairs, till you're all well again."

Katy tried to speak, but began to cry instead, which frightened Elsie very much.

"Does it hurt you so bad?" she asked, crying, too.

"Oh, no! It isn't that," sobbed Katy. "But I was so cross to you this morning, Elsie, and I pushed you. Oh, please forgive me, please do!"

"Why, it's got well," said Elsie, surprised. "The bump all went away."

"Oh, Elsie. Come here and kiss me."

Katy held out her arms. Elsie ran right into them, and

the big sister and the little hugged closer than they ever had before.

"You're the most *precious* little darling," murmured Katy, clasping Elsie tight. "I've been real horrid to you, Elsie. But I'll never be again. You shall play with me and Clover just as much as you like."

"Oh, goody, goody!" cried Elsie. "How sweet you are, Katy! I mean to love you next best to Cousin Helen and Papa!"

All the rest of the afternoon Elsie sat beside the bed with her palm-leaf fan, keeping off the flies and shooing away the other children when they peeped in at the door.

"I'll be so good to her when I get well," Katy thought to herself.

When morning came and Dr. Carr returned, he found her in a good deal of pain, hot, and restless.

"Papa!" she cried the first thing. "Must I lie here as much as a week?"

"My darling, I'm afraid you must," said her father, who looked worried.

"Dear, dear!" sobbed Katy. "How can I bear it?"

[7]

Dismal Days

❖

IF ANYBODY HAD told Katy that first afternoon that at the end of a week she would still be in bed, it would have almost killed her. She was so restless and eager that to lie still seemed one of the hardest things in the world.

Day after day she asked Papa, "Can I get up and go downstairs this morning?" And when he shook his head, the tears would come. But if she tried to get up it hurt her so much that she was glad to sink back again on the soft pillows and mattress.

Then there came a time when Katy didn't even ask to be allowed to get up. A time when sharp, dreadful pain, such as she had never imagined before, took hold of her. When days and nights got all confused and tangled up together, and Aunt Izzie never seemed to go to bed. A time when Papa was constantly in her room. It was all like a long, bad dream from which she couldn't wake up, though she tried ever so hard.

But by and by the pain grew less, and Katy began to take more notice of what was going on about her. "How long have I been ill?" she asked Papa one day.

"It is four weeks yesterday," he answered.

"Four weeks!" said Katy. "Why, I didn't know it was so long as that. Was I very sick, Papa?"

"Very, dear. But you are a great deal better now."

"How did I hurt myself when I tumbled out of the swing?" asked Katy.

"Well, did you know that you have a long bone down your back called your spine?"

"Yes, I think so," said Katy.

"It is made up of a row of smaller bones, and in the middle of it is a sort of rope of nerves called the spinal cord. Nerves, you know, are the things we feel with. Well, this spinal cord is rolled up for safekeeping in a soft wrapping called a membrane. When you fell out of the swing, you bruised the membrane inside, and the nerve inflamed and gave you a fever in the back. Do you see?"

"A little," said Katy, not quite understanding, but too tired to ask further. After she had rested awhile, she said, "Is the fever well now, Papa? Can I get up again and go downstairs right away?"

"Not right away, I'm afraid," said Dr. Carr, trying to speak cheerfully.

Katy didn't ask any more questions then. Another week passed, and another. The pain was almost gone. It only came back now and then for a few minutes. She could sleep now, and eat, and be raised in bed without feeling giddy. But still her legs hung heavy and lifeless, and she was not able to walk, or even stand alone.

"My legs feel so odd," she said, one morning. "What do you suppose is the reason, Papa? Won't they feel natural soon?"

"Not soon," answered Dr. Carr. "I am afraid, my darling, that you must make up your mind to stay in bed a long time."

"How long?" said Katy, looking frightened. "A month more?"

"I can't tell exactly how long," answered her father. "The doctors think, as I do, that the injury to your spine is one you will outgrow by and by, because you are so young and strong. But it may take a good while to do it. It may be that you will have to lie here for months, or it may be more. The only cure for such a hurt is time and patience. It is hard, darling, but you have hope to help you along."

Now that Katy knew there was no chance of getting well at once, the days dragged dreadfully.

Each seemed duller and more dismal than the day before. Katy lost heart about herself and took no interest in anything. Aunt Izzie brought her books, but she didn't want to read. The other children would come to sit with her, but hearing about the things they had been doing made her cry so miserably that Aunt Izzie wouldn't let them come often. They were very sorry for Katy, but the room was so gloomy and Katy was so cross that they didn't mind much not being allowed to see her.

In those days Katy made Aunt Izzie keep the blinds shut tight, and she would lie in the dark, thinking how miserable she was. Everybody was very kind and patient with her, but she was too selfishly miserable to notice it.

The first thing to break into this sad state of affairs was the news that Cousin Helen was coming for another short visit. For a week Katy was feverish with excitement, until at last Cousin Helen came. This time Katy was not on the steps to welcome her, but after a little while Papa brought Cousin Helen in his arms and sat her in a big chair beside the bed.

"How dark it is," Cousin Helen said, after they had kissed each other and talked for a minute or two. "I can't see your face at all. Would it hurt your eyes to have a little more light?"

"Oh, no," answered Katy. "It doesn't hurt my eyes,

only I hate to have the sun come in. It makes me feel worse somehow."

"I'll open the blind a little bit then," she said. "Now I can see."

Katy's face had grown thin, and her eyes had red circles about them from continual crying. Her hair had been brushed twice that morning by Aunt Izzie, but Katy had run her fingers through it till it stood out above her head like a bush. She wore a clean but ugly dressing gown, and the room, though tidy, had a dismal look.

"Isn't it horrid?" sighed Katy, as Cousin Helen looked around. "Everything's horrid. But I don't mind so much now that you've come. Oh, Cousin Helen, I've had such a dreadful, *dreadful* time!"

"I know," said her cousin. "I've heard all about it, Katy, and I'm very sorry for you! It is a hard trial, my poor darling."

"But how do you do it?" cried Katy. "How do you manage to be so sweet and beautiful and patient when you're feeling badly all the time and can't do anything, or walk, or stand?"

Cousin Helen didn't say anything for a little while. She just sat and stroked Katy's hand.

"Katy," she said at last, "has your papa told you that he thinks you are going to get well by and by?"

"Yes," replied Katy, "he did say so. But perhaps it won't be for a long, long time. And I want to do so many things. And now I can't do anything at all!"

"What sort of things?"

"Study, and help people, and become famous. And I wanted to teach the children. Mama said I must take care of them, and I meant to. And now I can't go to school or learn anything myself. And if ever I do get well, the children will be almost grown up and they won't need me."

"But why must you wait till you get well?" asked Cousin Helen, smiling.

"Why, Cousin Helen, what can I do lying here in bed?"

"A good deal. Shall I tell you, Katy, what it seems to me that I should say to myself if I were in your place?"

"Yes, please," replied Katy.

"I should say this: 'Now, Katy Carr, you wanted to go to school, and learn to be wise and useful, and here's a chance for you. But this is a different kind of school.'"

"But what is the school?" asked Katy. "I don't know what you mean."

"It is called 'the School of Patience,'" replied Cousin Helen. "And the place where the lessons are to be learned is this room of yours. The rules of the school are pretty hard, and the lessons aren't easy either, but the more you study the more interesting they become."

"What are the lessons?" asked Katy, beginning to feel as if Cousin Helen were telling her a story.

"Well, there's the lesson of Patience, of course. That's one of the hardest studies. You can't learn much of it at a time, but every bit you learn by heart makes the next bit easier. And there's the lesson of Cheerfulness. And the lesson of Making the Best of Things."

"But sometimes there isn't anything to make the best of," said Katy sadly.

"Yes, there is, almost always! You always can find an opportunity to learn and become a better person."

"If I only could!" sighed Katy. "Are there any other studies in the school, Cousin Helen?"

"Yes, there's the lesson of Hopefulness. And there is one final lesson, Katy—the lesson of Neatness. Schoolrooms must be kept in order, you know. A sick person ought to be as fresh and dainty as a rose. It will make *you* feel better, and it will make your visitors happier, too. Although you may be ill, you must think of others, too."

Katy now looked bright and eager. "Do you really think I could do so?" she asked.

"Do what? Comb your hair?"

"Oh, no! Be nice and sweet and patient, and a comfort to people. You know what I mean."

"I am sure you can, if you try."

"But what would you do first?" asked Katy, who was eager to begin.

"Well, first I would open the blinds and make the room look a little less dismal. Are you taking all those medicines in the bottles now?"

"No, only that big one with the blue label."

"Then you might ask Aunt Izzie to take away the others. And I'd get Clover to pick a bunch of fresh flowers every day for your table. By the way, I don't see the little white vase."

"No. It got broken the very day after you went away—the day I fell out of the swing," said Katy.

"Never mind, pet, don't look so sad. I know the tree those vases grow upon, and you shall have another. Then after the room is made pleasant, I would have all my lesson-books fetched up, if I were you, and I would study a couple of hours every morning."

"Oh!" cried Katy, making a face at the idea.

Cousin Helen smiled. "I know. It sounds like dull work, learning geography and Latin up here all by yourself. But if you make the effort, you'll be glad by and by. You won't lose so much ground, you see—won't slip back quite so far in your education."

"Well," said Katy, "I'll try. But it won't be a bit nice studying without anybody to study with me. Is there anything else, Cousin Helen?"

"You were saying just now that one of the things you were sorry about was that you could be of no use to the children. Do you know, I don't think you have that reason for being sorry."

"Why not?" said Katy.

"Because you *can* be of use. It seems to me that you have more of a chance with the children now than you ever could have had when you were well."

"I can't think what you mean," said Katy sadly. "Why, Cousin Helen, half the time I don't even know where they are or what they are doing. And I can't get up and go after them, you know."

"But you can make your room such a delightful place that they will want to come to you! Don't you see, a sick person has one thing going for her—she is always on hand. Everybody who wants her knows just where to go. If people love her, she gets naturally to be the heart of the house."

"Oh, Cousin Helen, you can't think how much better I feel. I *will* try!"

"It won't be easy," said her cousin. "There will be days when your head aches and you feel cross and don't want to think of anyone but yourself. And there'll be other days when Clover and the rest will come in and you will be doing something else and will feel as if their coming was a bother. But you must remember that every time you forget and are impatient and selfish, you drive them away."

Just then Dr. Carr came in.

"Oh, Papa! You haven't come to take Cousin Helen, have you?" cried Katy.

"Indeed I have," said her father. "Cousin Helen looks tired."

For a minute Katy felt just like crying. But she choked back the tears. "Then this will be my first lesson in patience," she said to herself, giving her papa as cheerful a smile as she could.

[8]

A Merry Christmas

❈

"WHAT ARE THE children all doing today?" Katy asked Aunt Izzie. "I haven't seen them since breakfast."

"I don't know," she replied. "They're out somewhere. They'll be back before long, I guess."

Her voice sounded a little odd and mysterious, but Katy didn't notice it.

"I thought of such a nice plan yesterday," Katy said. "That was, that all of them should hang their stockings up here tomorrow night instead of the nursery. Then I could see them open their presents, you know. Could they, Aunt Izzie? It would be real fun."

"I don't believe there will be any objection," replied her aunt. She looked as if she were trying not to laugh.

It had been more than two months now since Cousin Helen went away, and winter had come. Snow was falling outdoors. Katy could see the thick flakes go whirling past the window, but her room was warm and cozy. It was a pleasant room now. There was a bright fire in the grate. Everything was neat and orderly, the air was sweet with the perfume of flowers, and the Katy who lay in bed was a very different Katy from the sad girl of the last chapter.

Cousin Helen's visit, though it lasted only one day, did great good. Not that Katy grew perfect all at once. None of us do that, even in books. But Katy's feet were on the right path.

"I wish I had something pretty to put into everybody's stocking," Katy said. "But I've only got the scarf for Papa, and these mittens for Phil." She took them from under her pillow as she spoke. She had knitted them herself, a very little bit at a time.

"There's my pink sash," she said, suddenly. "I might give that to Clover. I only wore it once, you know, and I don't *think* I got any spots on it. Would you please fetch it and let me see, Aunt Izzie? It's in the top drawer."

Aunt Izzie brought the sash. It was quite fresh, and they both decided it would do nicely for Clover.

"I wish I had something real nice for Elsie. What she wants most of all is a writing desk. And Johnnie wants a sled. But, oh, dear! Those are such big things. And I've only got two dollars and a quarter."

Aunt Izzie marched out of the room without saying anything. When she came back, she had something folded up in her hand.

"I didn't know what to give you for Christmas, Katy," she said. "So I thought I'd give you this and let you choose for yourself. But if you've set your heart on getting presents for the children, perhaps you'd rather have it now." So saying, Aunt Izzie laid on the bed a crisp, new five-dollar bill!

"How good you are!" cried Katy. And indeed, Aunt Izzie did seem to have grown wonderfully good of late. Or rather, Katy at last saw the goodness in her aunt that had always been there.

Now Katy could afford to be generous. She gave Aunt Izzie an exact description of the desk she wanted for Elsie.

"It's no matter about its being very big," said Katy. "But it must have a blue velvet lining, and an inkstand with a silver top. And please buy some sheets of paper and envelopes and a pen—the prettiest you can find. Oh! And there must be a lock and key. Don't forget that, Aunt Izzie."

Katy thought for a moment. "I'd like the sled for Johnnie to be green and to have a nice name. 'Sky-Scraper' would be nice if there was one. And if there's money enough left, Aunty, won't you buy me a real nice book for Dorry, and a silver thimble for Clover? Oh! And some candy. I think that's all!"

Was ever seven dollars and a quarter expected to do so much? But the next day Aunt Izzie brought all the precious bundles into Katy's room. How Katy enjoyed untying the strings!

Everything was exactly right.

"There wasn't any 'Sky-Scraper,'" said Aunt Izzie, "so I got 'Snow-Skimmer' instead."

"It's beautiful, and I like it just as well," said Katy.

Katy was thinking so much about these presents that she barely noticed that none of the other children had been in her room for several days. However, after supper that night they all came up together, looking very merry, and as if they had been having a good time somewhere.

"You don't know what we've been doing!" said Philly.

"Hush, Phil!" said Clover. She divided the stockings, which she held in her hand, and everybody hung one up.

Then they all sat down around the fire to write their wishes to Santa Claus and chattered about the presents they hoped for. But soon Aunt Izzie came in and swept them all off to bed.

"I know how it will be in the morning," she said. "You'll all be up and racing about as soon as it's light. So you must get your sleep now, if ever."

After they had gone, Katy remembered that nobody

had offered to hang a stocking up for her. She felt a little hurt when she thought of it. "But I suppose they forgot," she said to herself.

A little later Papa and Aunt Izzie came in, and they filled the stockings. It was great fun. Each was brought to Katy, as she lay in bed, so that she could arrange it as she liked.

The toes were stuffed with candy and oranges. Then came the parcels, all shapes and sizes, tied in white paper with ribbons, and labeled.

The desk and sled were too big to go into any stocking, so they were wrapped in paper and hung beneath the other things. It was ten o'clock before all was done, and Papa and Aunt Izzie went away. Katy lay a long time watching the stockings as they dangled in the firelight. Then she fell asleep.

It seemed only a minute before something touched her and woke her up. It was Philly in his nightgown, climbing up on the bed to kiss her. The rest of the children, half dressed, were dancing about with their stockings in their hands. It was daytime already!

"Merry Christmas! Merry Christmas!" they cried. "Oh Katy, such beautiful, *beautiful* things!"

"Oh!" screamed Elsie, who at that moment saw her desk. "Oh, Katy, it's so sweet, and I'm so happy!" and Elsie hugged Katy.

But what was that strange thing beside the bed? Katy stared and rubbed her eyes. It certainly had not been there when she went to sleep. How had it come?

It was a little evergreen tree planted in a red flower-pot. The pot had stripes of gold paper stuck on it, and gold stars and crosses, which made it look very gay. The branches were hung with oranges and nuts and shiny red apples and popcorn balls and strings of bright berries. A number of little packages, tied with blue and red ribbon, also hung from the branches and looked so pretty that Katy gave a cry of delighted surprise.

"It's a Christmas tree for you!" said the children, all trying to hug her at once.

"We made it ourselves," said Dorry. "I pasted the stars on the pot."

"And I popped the corn," cried Philly.

"Do you like it?" asked Elsie, cuddling close to Katy.

Katy's eyes were brimming with happy tears.

"But you didn't notice what the tree's standing upon," said Clover.

It was a chair, a very large and curious one, with a long cushioned back that ended in a footstool.

"That's Papa's present," said Clover. "See, it tips back so as to be just like a bed. And Papa says he thinks pretty soon you can lie on it by the window, where you can see us play."

"Does he really?" said Katy, doubtfully. It still hurt her very much to be touched or moved.

"And see what's tied to the arm of the chair," said Elsie. It was a little silver bell with "Katy" engraved on the handle.

"Cousin Helen sent it. It's for you to ring when you want anybody to come," explained Elsie.

"How perfectly lovely everything is!" said Katy.

That was a pleasant Christmas. The children declared it to be the nicest they had ever had. And Katy thought so, too.

[9]

A New Lesson

❈

THE HOLIDAYS HAD brought some excitement to Katy's life, but as the winter and then spring months went by, one after another in procession, Katy's spirits began to sag again. Time seemed to drag for the poor girl stuck in her room.

"I wish something would happen," she often said to herself. And something was about to happen—but not something she would have wished for.

"Katy!" said Clover, coming in one day. "Do you know where the headache medicine is? Aunt Izzie has got *such* a headache."

"No," replied Katy. "I don't. Perhaps it's in Papa's room."

"How very odd!" she thought to herself, when Clover

was gone. "I never knew Aunt Izzie to have a headache before."

"How is Aunt Izzie?" she asked, when Papa came in at noon.

"She has some fever and a bad pain in her head. I have told her that she had better lie still and not try to get up this evening."

It seemed strange when the next day, and the next, and the next after that, passed and still no Aunt Izzie came near her. Katy began to appreciate for the first time how much she had learned to love her aunt. She missed her dreadfully.

"When is Aunt Izzie going to get well?" she asked her father. "I want her so much."

"We all want her," said Dr. Carr.

"Is she very ill?" asked Katy.

"I'm afraid so," he replied.

Aunt Izzie's attack proved to be a typhoid fever. The doctors said that the house must be kept quiet, so the children were sent to the neighbors' to stay.

They were all concerned for Aunt Izzie and hoping that she would get well soon. But it never occurred to the children that perhaps Aunt Izzie might not get well. So it came as a sudden shock to the children when one morning Papa came to tell them that Aunt Izzie had died in the night.

For the first time the Carr children realized what a good friend Aunt Izzie had been to them. Her worrying ways were all forgotten now. They could only remember the many kind things she had done for them since they were little. How they wished that they had never teased her, never said sharp words about her to each other!

"What shall we do without Aunt Izzie?" thought Katy as she cried herself to sleep that night. And the question came into her mind again and again after the funeral was over.

For several days she saw almost nothing of her father.

But after tea one day, Dr. Carr came upstairs to sit awhile in Katy's room. He often did so, but this was the first time since Aunt Izzie's death.

"I've been thinking how we are to manage about the housekeeping," said Dr. Carr, looking tired and sad. "Of course we shall have to get somebody to come and take charge. But it isn't easy to find just the right person."

"Oh, Papa!" cried Katy. "Must we have anybody?"

"Why, how do you suppose we are going to arrange it? Clover is much too young for housekeeping. And besides, she is at school all day."

"I don't know. Let me think about it," said Katy. And that evening she did.

"Papa," she said the next morning, "I've been thinking over what you were saying, about getting somebody to keep the house, you know. And I wish you wouldn't. I wish you would let *me* try."

"But how?" asked Dr. Carr. "I really don't see. If you were well and strong, perhaps. But even then, you would be pretty young, Katy."

"I shall be fourteen in two weeks," said Katy. "And if I *were* well, Papa, I should be going to school, you know, and then of course I couldn't. No, I'll tell you my plan. Our cook has been with us so long that she knows Aunt Izzie's ways. Now why couldn't she come up to me when anything is needed, instead of my going down to her? Do let me try! It will be real nice to have something to think about as I sit up here alone. Please say yes, Papa."

Dr. Carr thought it was a great deal too much for Katy, but he said, "Well, darling, you may try if you wish."

But Dr. Carr was wrong. At the end of the month Katy was eager to go on. So he said, "Very well, you may try it till spring."

Each day, as soon as breakfast was over and the dishes were washed and put away, Debby, the cook, would tie on a clean apron and come upstairs for orders. At first Katy thought this great fun. But after ordering dinner a good many times it began to grow tiresome, and it was hard to think of new things for Debby to make.

So Katy would read every cookbook in the house, till

she felt as if she had swallowed twenty dinners. And she would drive Debby crazy with all the new recipes she found.

Poor Debby! If she hadn't loved Katy so dearly, she might have lost her patience. And Dr. Carr had to eat a great many odd things in those days. But he didn't mind. As for the children, they enjoyed it. Dinnertime became quite exciting when nobody could tell exactly what any dish on the table was made of.

After a while Katy grew wiser. She stopped forcing Debby to try new things, and the Carr family went back to their usual roast beef and boiled ham and vegetables for dinner.

Month by month Katy learned how to manage a little better, and things began to go more and more smoothly. Dr. Carr watched her face grow brighter and decided that the experiment was a success.

[10]

Two Years Later

❖

IT WAS A PLEASANT morning in early June. A warm wind was rustling the trees. Dr. Carr's front door stood wide open, and through the parlor window came the sound of piano practice. On the steps, under the budding roses, sat a small figure busily sewing.

This was Clover—little Clover still, though more than two years had passed, and she was now fourteen. Her eyes were as blue and sweet as ever, and her cheeks as pink. But her brown pigtails were pinned up into a round knot, and her childish face looked almost womanly.

Soon the side gate swung open, and Philly came around the corner of the house. He had grown into a big boy. All his pretty baby curls had been cut off, and he now wore a jacket and trousers. In his hand he held something that Clover could not see.

"What's that?" she asked, as he reached the steps.

"I'm going to ask Katy if these are ripe," he answered, holding out a handful of plums.

"What did Phil want?" asked Elsie, opening the parlor door as Phil went upstairs.

"Only to know if the plums are ripe enough to eat. Have you got through practicing? It doesn't seem like an hour yet."

"Oh, it isn't. It's only twenty-five minutes. But Katy told me not to sit more than half an hour at a time without getting up and running around a bit."

Just then a tinkle sounded upstairs. "There's her bell!" said Clover. "I'll go see what she wants."

"No, let me go. I'll see!" But Clover was already halfway across the hall, and the two girls ran up side by side, as Phil came down, biting into a plum.

There was often a little battle over who should answer Katy's bell. All the children liked to wait on her so much.

Katy came to meet them as they entered, but not on her feet. That was still only a far-off possibility. She was now in a chair with large wheels, with which she was rolling herself across the room. This wheelchair was a great comfort to her. Sitting in it, she could get to her closet and help herself to what she wanted without troubling anybody. It was only lately that she had been able to use it.

She met the girls with a bright smile as they came in, and said, "Oh, Clover, after the carpet is put down, would you please dust Papa's desk?"

"Of course I will!" said Clover, who loved to help Katy in any way she could.

"Elsie, dear, run into Papa's room and bring me the drawer out of his table. I want to put that in order myself."

Elsie went cheerfully. She laid the drawer across Katy's lap, and Katy began to dust and arrange the contents.

Somebody tapped at the door. Katy called out, "Come in!" and in marched a tall young man with a solemn, sensible face, carrying a little clock carefully in both his hands.

This was Dorry. He had grown and improved very much and was turning out to be quite clever. Among other things, he had developed a talent for mechanics.

"Here's your clock, Katy," he said. "I've got it fixed so that it strikes all right."

"Have you really?" said Katy. "Why, Dorry, you're a genius! Thank you so much."

"It's just about eleven now," went on Dorry, "so it'll strike pretty soon."

Just then the clock began to strike.

"There," Dorry said. "That's splendid, isn't it?"

But alas! The clock did not stop at eleven. It went on—twelve, thirteen, fourteen, fifteen, sixteen!

"Dear me," said Clover. "What does all this mean? It must be the day after tomorrow, at least."

Dorry took the clock—shook it, slapped it, and turned it upside down. But still it kept on. At last, at the one-hundred-and-thirtieth stroke, it suddenly stopped.

"It's very odd," he said, "but I'm sure it's not because of anything I did. I can fix it, though, if you'll let me try again. May I, Katy? I'll promise not to hurt it."

For a moment Katy hesitated. Clover pulled her sleeve and whispered, "Don't." But Katy had made up her mind.

"Yes! Take it, Dorry. I'm sure you'll be careful."

"Oh, thank you, Katy. I'll have this fixed for you in a jiff!"

"How come you let him take your clock again?" said Clover as soon as the door was shut. "He'll spoil it."

"I don't believe he'll hurt it," answered Katy, "and it'll be good for him to give it another try."

"You were real good to do it," responded Clover. "But if it had been mine, I don't think I could."

Just then the door flew open, and Johnnie rushed in, also two years taller, but otherwise looking exactly as she used to do.

"Oh, Katy!" she cried. "Won't you please tell Philly not to wash the chicks in the rainwater tub?"

"Why, he mustn't—of course he mustn't!" said Katy. "What made him think of such a thing?"

"He says they're dirty because they've just come out of their eggshells! And he insists that the yellow on them is egg yolk. I told him it wasn't, but he wouldn't listen to me." Johnnie wrung her hands.

"Clover!" cried Katy. "Won't you run down and ask Philly to come up to me?"

Clover ran out to fetch him, and soon Philly came up. Katy lifted him into her lap, which, big boy though he was, he liked extremely, and she explained to him about the poor little chicks.

"I didn't mean to hurt them," he said, "but they were all dirty and yellow—with egg, you know, and I thought you'd like me to clean them up."

"But that wasn't egg, Philly—it was clean little feathers, like a canary's wings."

"Was it?"

"Yes, and now the chickies are as cold as you would feel if you had tumbled into a pond and nobody gave you any dry clothes. Don't you think you ought to go and warm them?"

"But how?"

"Well, in your hands, very gently. And then let them run around in the sun."

"I will!" said Philly, getting down from her lap. "Only kiss me first, because I didn't mean to, you know!"

"Isn't Katy sweet?" said Johnnie to Clover, who was looking on from the hall.

"Isn't she!" replied Clover. "I wish I were half as good."

[11]

At Last

❈

ONE DAY ABOUT six weeks later Clover and Elsie heard the sound of Katy's bell ringing. Both ran up, two steps at a time, to see what she wanted.

Katy sat in her chair, looking flushed and excited.

"Oh, girls!" she cried. "What do you think? I stood up!"

"What?" cried Clover and Elsie.

"I really did! I stood up on my feet! By myself!"

The others were too surprised to speak.

"It was all at once, you see. Suddenly, I had the feeling that if I tried I could, and almost before I thought, I *did* try, and there I was, up and out of the chair. Only I kept hold of the arm all the time! Oh, girls!" And Katy buried her face in her hands.

"Do you think I shall ever be able to do it again?" she asked, looking up with wet eyes.

"Why, of course you will!" said Clover.

Katy tried, but now she could not move out of the chair at all. She began to wonder if she had dreamed the whole thing.

But the next day, when Clover happened to go into Katy's room, Katy was standing.

"Papa!" shrieked Clover, rushing downstairs. "Dorry, John, Elsie! Come and see!"

This time Katy found no trouble in doing it again. When Papa came in, he was as excited as any of the children. He walked around and around the chair, making Katy stand up and sit down.

"Am I really going to get well?" she asked.

"Yes, my love, I think you are," said Dr. Carr with a great smile. "I think it is coming, my darling, but it will take time. You must go very slowly."

"Oh, Papa," said Katy, "it's no matter if it takes a year—if only I get well at last."

How happy she was that night—too happy to sleep. Papa noticed the dark circles under her eyes in the morning and shook his head.

"You must be careful," he told her, "or you'll be laid up again. A fever now would put you back for years."

Katy knew Papa was right, and she was careful, though it was not easy. Her progress was slow. At first she stood on her feet only a few seconds, then a minute, then five minutes, holding tightly all the while by the chair. Next, she let go of the chair and stood alone. After that she began to walk a step at a time. No baby of a year old was ever prouder of her first steps than she.

One day she was able to walk out of her room and down the hall. In two or three weeks she was able to walk all over the second floor!

By the end of August she had grown so strong that she began to talk about going downstairs.

But Papa said, "Wait a bit. It will tire you much more than walking about on a level."

"I think so, too," said Clover. "And besides, a beautiful idea has come into my head! You shall fix a day to come down, Katy, and we'll be all ready for you and have a celebration. That would be just lovely! How soon may she, Papa?"

"Well, in ten days, let's say."

So it was settled. "How delicious!" cried Clover, skipping about and clapping her hands.

At last the day of the celebration came.

"Katy!" said Clover, as she came in from the garden with her hands full of flowers, "that dress of yours is sweet. You never looked so nice before in your life!" And she stuck a beautiful carnation to Katy's dress and fastened another in her hair.

"There," she said, "now you're ready. Papa is coming up in a few minutes to take you down."

Just then Elsie and Johnnie came in. They had on their best dresses. So did Clover.

And now Papa appeared. Very slowly they all went downstairs, Katy leaning on Papa, with Dorry on her other side, and the girls behind, while Philly went ahead.

"Oh, the front door is open!" said Katy. "How nice! And what a pretty tablecloth. That's new since I was here."

"Don't stop to look at *that*!" cried Philly, who seemed in a great hurry about something. "Come into the parlor instead."

"Yes!" said Papa. "Dinner isn't quite ready yet, so you'll have time to rest a little after your walk downstairs. Are you very tired, Katy?"

"Not a bit!"she replied. "I could do it alone, I think."

"Oh, come on!" cried Phil again.

So they moved on. Papa opened the parlor door. Katy took one step into the room, then stopped. What was it that she saw?

The sofa was pulled out, and there upon it lay—Cousin Helen! When she saw Katy, she held out her arms.

Katy, forgetting her weakness, let go of Papa's arm,

and absolutely *ran* toward the sofa. "Oh, Cousin Helen! Dear, dear Cousin Helen!" she cried. Then she tumbled down by the sofa somehow, the two pairs of arms and the two faces met, and for a moment or two not a word more was heard from anybody.

"Isn't it a nice surprise?" shouted Philly.

The happy thought of getting Cousin Helen to the celebration was Clover's. She had proposed it to Papa and had made all the arrangements.

"Cousin Helen's going to stay three weeks this time—isn't that nice?" asked Elsie. "Are you sure that you didn't suspect? Not one bit?"

"No, indeed—not the least. How could I suspect anything so perfectly delightful?" And Katy gave Cousin Helen another kiss.

Such a short day that seemed! There was so much to see, to ask about, to talk over, that the hours flew, and evening came like another great surprise.

"Dear Katy," Cousin Helen said, a day or two after her arrival, "this visit is a great pleasure to me—you can't think how great. Do you remember the last I made, when you were so sick and so sad?"

"Indeed I do! And how good you were, and how you helped me! I shall never forget that."

"I'm glad! But what I could do was very little. You have been learning by yourself all this time. And Katy, darling, I want to tell you how pleased I am to see how bravely you have worked your way up. I can see it in everything—in your papa, in the children, in yourself. You have done very well, my dear Katy."

"Oh, Cousin Helen, don't," said Katy, her eyes filling with tears. "I haven't been brave. You can't think how badly I sometimes have behaved—how cross and ungrateful I am, how stupid, and slow. Every day I see things that ought to be done, and I don't do them. It's too nice to have you praise me—but you mustn't. I don't deserve it."

But although she thought she didn't deserve it, Cousin Helen, Dr. Carr, and the children knew that Katy did.